MW00905144

MAGICAL JOURNEYS

A Collection of Short Stories on Friendship, Love and Trust

By

H.C. Hulme

authorHOUSE™

1663 LIBERTY DRIVE, SUITE 200
BLOOMINGTON, INDIANA 47403
(800) 839-8640
WWW.AUTHORHOUSE.COM

First published by AuthorHouse 12/08/05

ISBN: 1-4208-5212-4 (sc)
ISBN: 1-4208-5213-2 (dj)

Library of Congress Control Number: 2005904246

Printed in the United States of America
Bloomington, Indiana

This book is printed on acid-free paper.

This book is dedicated to all children, big or small; to my family and friends; and to one special person who made it all possible with his encouraging words!

Thank you from the bottom of my heart!

Acknowledgement:

I would like to take this time to acknowledge everyone who helped me with my book taking flight. First and foremost, I would like to thank, my family for the love, understanding and continuous support while during my absence from the real world. Secondly, I would like to say that regarding the editing of my book, it really shows where friendship lies. Thank you all for this generous offer. For the wonderful reviews that made the difference, love to you all. For all the late nights you have given, regarding the redoing of illustrations, just know how much I love you. And last but not least, to everyone else who had a part in this, there are not enough words to express my happiness because of you! God bless you all!

Table of Contents

The Adventures of Jack, Jig and Bangger

"Wait, wait for me! I want to come, too," screamed Bangger as he was chasing Jack and Jig.

"No, Bangger, we don't want you to come," said Jack, running faster to get away from him.

"Why?"

"You're too much trouble, and besides, our safety would always be at risk."

"Ah, come on, guys. I promise to behave. Please, please let me come," begged Bangger.

"Oh, Jack, what are we going to do?" asked Jig, staring off into space when they stopped for a rest.

"I don't know. I knew this was going to happen," sneered Jack. "We should have left to cross the border at 4:00 AM like I wanted to. But no, no, you had to get your eight hours of sleep."

"That's not fair, Jack; my mother told me I needed it. You know mothers are always right."

"Yeah, yeah, whatever!" said Jack.

"Well, what are we going to do? Are we going to let him come with us?"

"Gee, will you hush up for a minute and let me think," said Jack, tapping his foot and rolling his eyes, as he let out a big sigh. Growling to himself, Jack turned to Bangger and gave him the once-over. "I'm telling you, if you mess up just one time," he said, pointing his finger at him, "that's it; I'll send you on your way."

"You mean it, Jack? Really, I can come? Oh gosh, gee golly, I'm going with the boys; I'm going with the boys," said Bangger, clapping his hands and bouncing up and down. "Thanks, guys. It's just going to be like old times, ain't it, Jack?"

"Bangger, the proper word is, isn't not ain't," yelled Jig.

"Why don't the both of you quiet down for a while and let me think how we are going to cross over the border," said Jack, sounding annoyed.

"We could say we live there and we're on our way home," said Bangger.

"We can't."

"Why?"

"Because, nitwit, you've got to have an address or passport, and that's something we don't have."

"We can make one up. They won't check, will they?"

"Oh! I can just feel it now; I know I'm going to live to regret this," answered Jack as he clenched his teeth and ran his fingers through his hair. "Bangger, why don't you go over to the grocery store and buy a block of cheese, and make sure you put it on ice.

We've got a long way to go, and there's nothing worse than moldy cheese."

"Okay, I can do that, Jack; I really can. Consider it done. I'm on my way."

As Bangger headed for the store, Jack and Jig were in a deep discussion as to how they were going to cross over the bridge from one country to another.

"I think we should wait until we see a lady open her purse and then jump in," said Jig.

"No, I don't think so. Sometimes they open it a thousand times just to get a look at themselves in the mirror. I don't get that concept at all," answered Jack, rubbing his head. "Surely they really don't think they are going to change in ten minutes. Do you think?"

"Actually, Jack, I was thinking more about salvaging some of our food. You know, sometimes ladies carry chocolate bars in their purses, and we could feast on that and save our cheese."

"Yeah, well, you're right about that, but if someone put her hand in her purse and got pricked by my rake, she would freak. And if she saw us, I don't want to think what would happen next. We might just get a free ride over the falls in an undesirable way."

"Oh yeah, and I can't swim," said Jig, fidgeting with his ear. "What are we going to do, Jack, huh, what?"

"Why is it always me that has to come up with all the answers? Can't you think of anything?"

"Well, sure I can. Maybe we could dance our way over. You know, doing the jig.

Everybody likes entertainment."

"I think you had better save that for when we get over to the other side because it might keep us from starving when we run out of money."

"Where is that pain in the rear? He should have been back by now. Honestly, if he is into trouble, this is where he stays."

A few minutes passed, and Jig noticed Bangger coming back.

"Jack, look; who is that with Bangger?"

"I don't know. All I can say is, it had better not be a police dog, or he is out."

"Who's your friend, Bangger?" asked Jig, winking at Jack.

"Would you look at that, Clyde; see the look on their faces? They're already thinking I messed up. Just to let you boys know, I, Bangger Buddles, have gotten us a free ride over to the great north land."

"Well, I'm impressed," Jack said sheepishly as he fumbled with his fingers behind his back.

Jig approached Clyde and made a quick introduction and said, "Thank you," and gave him a pat on the head.

"Very nice to meet you, Clyde," said Jack, "but how did he convince you to do this?"

"Well, it didn't take much coaxing when he mentioned cheese. I may be a bloodhound, but there ain't anything like a bite of cheddar."

"Ah, excuse me, but I believe the word is isn't, not ain't."

"You could be right about that, but I'm not going to argue with you. I just know my job is to chase hare and fox and maybe a raccoon now and then. As long as I get fed, what do I care if I have schooling? Hey, Buddy!"

"His name is Bangger."

"Oh yeah, right! Where's that cheese? Sure could do with a bite or two before we check out of here. Ah! The taste, the smell, there's nothing like it. Thanks, Buddy, I mean, Bangger."

"So, what's your plan? How are we going to do this?" asked Jig.

"This is how I figured you could reach the other side without anyone noticing. When my master puts my backpack on me, I will purposely leave the zipper open and sit by the bench near the booth. He usually lets me do my business while he shows my papers inside. We'll have to work very fast to make sure you guys are right there on time to jump in before he comes back. Once you're inside, it's smooth sailing from here on out."

"It sounds good, but I'm wondering if you have noticed the felines with their noses high over there? You know they can smell mice a mile away, and I don't care to be someone's dinner tonight," said Jig.

"You worry too much." Clyde smiled, shaking his head.

"That's okay for you to say; they don't want to eat you," answered Jig.

"Hey listen; I'm going to give you guys a head start, about thirty minutes. You guys run up ahead and hide behind that garbage can and watch for me.

When you see me flick my right ear, that means head over to the bench, okay?

You'll have about seven minutes to climb up on my back and get settled in my backpack. And for goodness sake, try not to pull the fur out."

"Relax, all we want is a ride," answered Jack, sounding annoyed.

"Oh and please don't use the rake. If that gets stuck in my fur and I howl, just remember it's going to draw attention, and that's something we want to avoid. By the way, I was going to ask you, why do you carry that rake with you? Is it a good luck charm or something?"

"No. It's not a good luck charm. During summer vacation in the past, I worked raking lawns and did a few other jobs, but this seemed to pay the best. I carry it with me just incase I need to earn more money. It gives me a little in my pocket, and it puts food in my belly. What more could I ask for?"

"I don't know," said Clyde, raising his eyebrows. "Sounds like too much work if you ask me. Where are you guys headed after we cross the bridge?"

"We're not really sure."

"What? Are you crazy?"

"No! Why?"

"No one in their right mind would do something like this and not have a destination."

"Haven't you ever wanted to have a little adventure in your life?" asked Jig.

"Yeah, but not like this. I mean, it would be nice to know where I would end up."

"Why? That takes all the fun out of it."

"I don't think so; I like to know where my bed is." Clyde walked away shaking his head in disbelief. "See you later, guys."

"Okay, bye!"

Chapter 2

Jack turned to Bangger and asked, "What did you pay for that cheese?"

"Um, well, you see, I was going to talk to you about that."

"Ah-ha, I knew it. We haven't even left here, and already you did something."

"Wait a minute; can I tell you what happened without you rambling on? Please, have a little faith."

"I would, but your track record hasn't been the best, has it?" smirked Jack.

"Well, for your information, I did very well in the grocery store. You see, there was a man who kept picking up all different kinds of cheeses, and one of the stickers fell off on the floor, and I just happened to pick it up."

"Right, and you got caught putting it over another label," said Jack, frowning.

"No, I did not," Bangger said as he held his head up as proud as a peacock. "The lady who was pricing the cheese said, 'Thank you,' and told me it was nice to see that there are still honest mice in the world. To show her appreciation, she gave me a big block of cheese for two dollars. Now what are you going to say, eh, Jacky boy! Bangger did well." He breathed on his fingers and rubbed them across his chest.

"All right, maybe this time, but we'll see how long it lasts."

"Gee, Jack; aren't you ever going to trust me?"

"Hey, you have to earn trust."

As Bangger walked away talking to himself, Jack whispered to Jig, snickering, "There might be hope for him yet."

"It's about time, Jack, that we started over to the garbage can," said Jig.

"Yeah right. Come on, let's go. Bangger, are you coming? It's time to go.

We better get a move on before Clyde gets here."

On the way over to the trash can, Jig decided to do a little dance. You could hear people laughing and having a good time watching him. Of course, at one point, he tripped over the crack in the sidewalk and landed on his backside.

One small child, a little girl, was so taken with him that she asked her mommy for money to give to him. It was then that a few other people saw this and reached into their pockets, too, for loose change. By the time they arrived at the trash can, Jig had finished his dance. As he took a bow, he said, 'Thank you,' and turned to Jack, who was already counting the money.

"Not bad, Jig; you must be getting better, or they feel sorry for you because of those ripped pair of trousers," said Jack.

"Meow!"

"Did you hear that, Jack?"

"Yeah, where is it?"

"I don't know. It's too close for comfort; I know that. Bangger, keep your eyes open. There's a puss-in-boots not too far off. Look, Jig, over to the right. Isn't that the bench we're supposed to wait by?"

"That's it."

"I'm telling you, I'm not going anywhere near there as long as Miss Whiskers is over there."

"Oh no, look! Here comes Clyde, and he's raising his ear. Now what are we going to do, Jack?"

"I don't know; why don't you think of something? Bangger, get over here. I was just thinking how much bigger and faster you are than both of us. Maybe you could go over there and, well, you know, scare that cat off."

"Yeah right. What do I look like? I've done a lot of things, Jack, but I'm not that stupid. In fact, just to let you know, while you two were over here arguing, I, on my own again, saved the day. I wrote a note to Clyde and held it up for him to read. Any minute now, he will be making a beeline for that cat. Well, isn't anybody going to say something?

Gosh, what's a guy got to do around here to get a little thank you?"

"You're really starting to bug me, Bangger."

"Come on, Jack; he's really trying."

"Okay, okay, thanks," mumbled Jack.

"That's it! That's all I'm getting? Hardly makes a fellow want to do anything else," said Bangger, shifting from side to side, folding his arms across his chest.

"Oh, come on, you two. Stop with the bickering. Is this whole trip going to be wasted on you two arguing all the time?"

"It wouldn't be if he would just watch his mouth," said Jack.

"Woof, woof!"

"There's Clyde. Wow, look at him go; he's fast, eh! Oh no! His master dropped the leash. Yikes, I can't look."

"Meow! Meow!"

"Tell me. No, don't tell me. Is that cat still alive?" questioned Jig, covering his eyes. "Did he get her?"

"No! Wow! That cat shimmied up that flagpole. She's hanging on to that flag as though it was her last meal. I've never seen anything like that before." said Jack.

"Jig, I didn't know you were squeamish." smiled Bangger.

"Well, I just haven't eaten yet today."

"Yeah right," said Bangger, smirking to himself.

"Bangger, knock it off. Come on; we have to go. Clyde's waiting for us. Follow me and stay close," said Jack.

Whispering to Jack, Jig said, "Do you see what's over there by the souvenir shop?"

"Yeah, I saw them about ten minutes ago."

"Jack, I'm frightened. Are we going to make it? Look at them; they look awfully hungry."

"Will you please stop talking and run? Hurry, keep up. We're almost there."

"Wow! I can't believe we made it," said Jig.

"Of course we made it; you have to have a little faith," said Jack.

"We made it," said Bangger, wiping the sweat from his brow.

"Where have you been? I just said that," replied Jig, waving his fist.

"Thank goodness, I can breathe. My heart feels like it's coming through my chest," said Jack.

"Hi, guys. Did you see that? I guess I put that cat in her place," laughed Clyde.

"Yes, thanks; but did you notice what's over there by the other shop?" asked Jig, pointing to his left.

"Where? What? Oh, now I see. Don't worry about that. I got that covered; one bark from me, and they'll wish they had jumped over the falls. Come on, fellows; we better get this done before my master comes out."

Chapter 3

"Jack, you go first and throw me down the shoelace that you found. It will be much easier if you use it to pull us up," said Jig.

"Okay. Hold still, Clyde."

"Gee, watch it; you're pulling. Ouch! Be careful," yelped Clyde.

"Quick! Give him a piece of cheese!"

"Cheese, where? Where's the cheese?"

"Hey, Jig, I'll bet if you give him a piece of cheese, he'll follow us anywhere. As a matter of fact," said Jack quietly, "I'll even bet my rake that if you give him a big enough piece of cheese, he'll take us anywhere."

"But, Jack, we've already talked about this and agreed we would be going our own way as soon as we cleared the bridge."

"Yeah, yeah, I know what I said; you don't have to remind me," grumbled Jack.

"That's it; just a little more. I'm almost there. Whoops!"

"Ouch! Watch it!" said Clyde.

"Sorry, Clyde. I didn't mean to hurt you. Oh no! My beautiful rake! I never knew fur balls were so tough. How did you get a fur ball with short hair? Gee, look at my rake."

"Jack, Jack, what's going on up there?"

"Nothing. I bent my rake." Jack frowned.

"Throw me down the shoelace," said Jig excitedly.

"Okay, here it comes."

"Have you got it?"

"Yes, now pull."

"For gosh sakes, will you please use your feet and help me? You climb as I pull."

"Oh! Okay, I get it."

"Wow, for a little guy, I didn't think you weighed so much."

"Well, Mother said—"

"Not now, Jig; we have to get Bangger up here, and that's going to take all of our strength."

"Howdy, guys!"

"Bangger, how did you get up here?"

"That was easy; I just asked Clyde to give me a lift with his paw."

"You really think you're something, don't you?"

"Hey, don't start, Jack."

"Well, he could have told us, and I wouldn't have bent my rake."

"Never mind, it's over. Come on in here; it's great. There's even a big dog chew in here. It's not the greatest. I've already tried it, but we could chew it up until it's mushy and use it for a pillow."

"This is good. All we need now is a television, and we'd be all set."

"Yes, you're right."

"Clyde, can you hear me?"

"Yeah, what do you want?"

"Well, I was just wondering; are you going to run fast like you did after that cat?" Jack smiled.

"Why?"

"Because, I don't want Bangger's brains scrambled like eggs, you know, from bouncing around too much," laughed Jack.

"One day, you're going to be sorry for all the nasty things you say, Jack." answered Bangger.

"Guys, hold on to the straps in the backpack while I jump up into the car," said Clyde.

"Hush, he's here. Get over to the right. Clyde's master is putting those papers in the small pocket," said Jack. "Okay, everyone be quiet."

Zip!

"Remember, just whisper; we don't want anyone looking in the backpack." said Jig.

"Okay, we got it." Bangger grinned.

"Hi there. Papers please!"

"Yes, sir."

"How long were you over here?"

"I was just visiting for the week."

"What was the nature of your business?"

"I was doing a little hunting at my brother's place."

"Is this your dog?"

"Yes, sir."

"He's a fine-looking animal."

"He sure is."

"Why does he have a backpack on?"

"Well, I figure he's got to earn his keep, too, so I make him carry his own bones and papers."

"That's really funny. Have you got anything to declare?"

"No, nothing."

"All right, you're free to go. Have a good day," said the border officer as he chuckled.

"Jack, did you hear that? We're here; I can't believe we actually did it." said Jig.

"You mean Clyde did it," muttered Jack.

"Excuse me! Who did it?"

"Gee, Bangger; are you ever going to stop?"

"You know, you're starting to give me a headache," said Jack.

"Sorry; all I want is a little recognition. I don't see the big deal with that," said Bangger, frowning.

"No, you're right; I'm sorry, and just for doing a great job today, I'll tell you what you can do."

"What's that, Jack?" said Bangger, all excited.

"You, my friend, can have the honor of scratching my back."

"That doesn't seem like a good reward, Jack."

"Jack, leave him alone," said Jig as he felt a little testy toward him for always ridiculing Bangger.

"How long do you think it will be before we stop, Clyde?"

"Probably within the next fifteen minutes.

My master usually stops just up ahead at the gas station on the right. When we get out of the car, he'll tie me to the post while he goes inside to fetch a coffee. That's when I'll pull the zipper down, and you guys can slide on out."

"Jack, I'm excited; are you?" questioned Jig.

"Yeah, I really didn't believe we would make it here."

"Why? Were you afraid those cats were going to eat us?"

"No, I just didn't think we would get over here, you know, on the other side of the border."

"Oh, look at Bangger; he's fast asleep. He must be tired."

"Yeah, I guess so."

"Jack, the car is slowing down. Wake up, Bangger."

"What, what's going on?" said Bangger, sitting up and rubbing his eyes.

"Come on, big guy; this is where we get off."

"Really, this is it?" asked Bangger, stretching.

"Okay, guys, time to hit the road."

Looking up at Clyde, Bangger wiped the tears from his eyes and said, "I'm going to miss you. I feel like I'm losing my best friend even though I've never had one."

"Ah, come on now, none of that. I can't be seen doing all this mushy stuff. I have an image to keep up. What do you think other dogs would say seeing me like this? Okay, just one quick hug. That's it; that's enough. Don't mess the fur."

"I know how you feel, Bangger. I feel the same way. Will we ever see you again?" asked Jig in between sobs.

"All right! That's enough. Come on, guys; we got to go. Hey, Clyde, thanks for everything, and I hope you don't get too constipated from eating all that cheese. If you do, just chew on a couple pieces of rhubarb; that will soon move things along." Jack smiled.

"Yeah, okay, Jack; thanks for the tip," Clyde said as he waved his paw. "Bye, guys. Hope to see you sometime. If you're ever north of the big city, look me up. I'm in the book under 'Clyde's Bloodlines.'"

"See you!"

"Bye, and thanks again." yelled Bangger.

Chapter 4

"Well, guys, here we are. It's exciting, isn't it?" asked Jack.

"Sure is. I don't know about you guys, but I'm really hungry," said Jig, rubbing his belly. "Jack, Bangger, what do you say we stop over there at the picnic tables and have a bite to eat?"

"Sounds like a plan to me," said Bangger, "and I need to use that washroom, too."

"Look, fellows, we have to make some plans before we go any further," said Jack.

"I thought we were just flying by the seat of our pants?" asked Bangger.

"Well, we are, but I was thinking we should have a couple of backup plans, you know, just in case."

"In case of what, Jack?"

"Just in case we need them."

"So, I take it you were listening to Clyde, in a roundabout way." Bangger smiled.

"Will you please do something? Go and eat, or take a walk. You might want to gather up a few branches for tonight. I heard it can get quite chilly up here at nighttime.

We'll stay here for tonight, and I will make a small fire to keep us warm," said Jack.

"Are we sleeping outside tonight, Jack?" questioned Jig, expressing fear.

"Jig, do you see a Mouse Inn around here anywhere?" said Jack sarcastically.

"No."

"Well then, of course we are.

"But I've never slept outside other than in my backyard, Jack. We're not wild mice or rats. We're domesticated, and we don't know what's out here."

"Ah, come on; you're not going to turn yellow on me now. Are you?"

"Hey, guys, look what I found."

"Where did you find that, Bangger?" asked Jack.

"I found it over there by the tree stump."

"It fits you very well."

"Yes it does. I've always wanted a cowboy hat. All I need now is the shoelace you had, and I could pretend to rope cows. Have you still got it, Jack?"

"Yes, it's here somewhere."

"Can I have it please?"

"Yes, okay, just a minute."

While Jack was rummaging through his potato sack looking for the shoelace, Jig sat nervously thinking about his warm bed at home. Interrupting his thoughts, Jig heard Jack say, "Seeing how Bangger came without a blanket, you can share yours with him."

"Okay," said Jig. "I don't mind."

Jig felt better knowing there would be someone nearby. He also figured that if anything was going to come after them, it would go for the bigger guy while he had time to run.

Turning to Jack, Jig said, "I think I'll retire for the night. I think we all should; it's been a long day."

"I'll start the fire; you two go ahead. Good night, fellows."

"Good night, Jack."

"Jack, do you think you could sing that song, you know, the one about the buffalo and the range?" said Bangger.

"Do you mean 'Home on the Range?'"

"Yes, that's it."

"It sure would make it a little easier to fall asleep being out here in the middle of nowhere, hearing all those funny little sounds and all." said Bangger.

"Okay, sure, I'll sing it." Jack cleared his throat. "Home, home on the range, where the deer and the antelope play. Where seldom is heard—"

Crack!

"Jack, what's that? Jacky, I'm scared!"

Whispering to Jig, Bangger said, "Don't worry; I'm a big guy, and no one is going to mess with me."

"Howdy, folks; just passing through and saw your fire. Can I warm my toes?"

"Who are you?" asked Jack.

"The name is Firecracker."

"Firecracker, what kind of name is that?"

"What do you mean?"

"Well, it's not normal."

"Who's to say what's normal? What's your name?"

"Jack."

"Ah, like Jack and the Beanstalk."

"No, just Jack."

"Well, who says that's normal?"

"I say!"

"Oh no; that guy doesn't know it, but it's not good to get under Jack's skin," Jig whispered to Bangger.

Throwing off the blanket, Jig got up and asked Jack to let Firecracker warm his feet. "Come on, Jacky; he'll be gone soon."

"Hey, fellows, guess what I just thought," yelled Bangger.

"What?" They both turned around and glared at him.

"I'm Bangger, and he's Firecracker, and we could make an explosion. Pretty good, eh, Jacky!" said Bangger, laughing. "I just told my first joke in a new country."

"Go to sleep, Bangger."

"Fine! I was just trying to lighten up the mood. Good night."

"You fellows are not from around here, are you?"

"I think you just heard Bangger say that," replied Jack, sounding testy.

"So, you're here from the south? What are you doing here?"

"Are you a cop or just writing a book? And if you really must know, we are on an adventure."

"An adventure? I've always wanted to go on one."

"Yeah, well, start now; there's the road."

"I don't suppose I could tag along with you fellows, could I?"

"No! Definitely not!"

"Ah, come on, guys; I could show you around and take you to a place where there's always free food."

"Free food!" said Jack, glaring at Firecracker.

"Yes, for sure; you can eat there all day and not have the same thing twice. The best part is it's still warm when you get it. I got it all right up here," he said as he pointed to his head. "They throw the food out every eight minutes."

"What? That doesn't sound right to me," said Jack, staring at Firecracker. "The humans do this?"

"Yes; who said humans were right? If you let me stay, I'll take you there in the morning. What do you say, guys?"

"You stay here; Jig and I will have a talk and let you know," answered Jack.

"Okay, thanks."

While Jack and Jig were conversing, and Firecracker was warming his feet,

Bangger was slowly counting stars while falling asleep.

After a few minutes, Jack and Jig went back over to the fire and told Firecracker he could stay for the night. In the morning, they would decide after they tasted a warm breakfast whether or not they would let him tag along for a while.

"Just one more thing: I don't share my blanket with anyone, got it?" said Jack.

"Hey, no problem; I've got my flannels on," said Firecracker, giggling.

"Oh, another thing: Don't try robbing us in the night. I've got my rake right here beside me."

"I wouldn't want to do that, Jack," laughed Firecracker. "I have a feeling this could be the start of a wonderful friendship."

"Yeah, well, we'll see about that. Good night."

"Good night!"

Chapter 5

"Mousy boo bah, mousy bay, I can just tell it's going to be a cheesy day."

"Bangger, what are you doing?"

"Ah, good morning, Jacky. Did you sleep well?"

Clenching his teeth, Jack said, "Number one, it is six o'clock in the morning, and number two, you are not a rooster. You are a MOUSE! Now go back to bed."

"Sorry, Jacky, no can do. I have been up with the birds and found wild gooseberries and have already got a head start on breakfast."

"For your information, we are having a warm breakfast today."

"Nobody told me, but then why would anybody? I'm just a nothing around here."

"Don't start, Bangger."

"Hey, what's all that noise about?" asked Jig, yawning.

"Nothing; go back to sleep," answered Jack.

Stretching and buzzing, Firecracker woke up. "Well, well, I see we're getting an early start. You weren't leaving without me, were you?"

"Don't you start. I may have to put up with him, but I won't with you," said Jack.

"Gee, are you always this grumpy?" asked Firecracker.

"No, most times he's worse," laughed Bangger.

"You've had it now, Bangger. Wait until I get a hold of you," said Jack as he started to chase Bangger around the big pine tree.

"Bangger! Jack! That's it! I am not going to stay here any longer listening to the two of you. I'm going home."

Bangger stopped dead in his tracks, and Jack ran into him.

"Hey, Jig, come on; we didn't come this far to turn back now," said Jack.

"Yeah, Jig."

"I'm sorry; I can't deal with this commotion all the time. If I wanted to hear it, I might as well of stayed at home. This isn't fun anymore," said Jig with his head down, crying.

Firecracker handed Jig a tissue and gave him a pat on his back.

"Gee, Jig, I'm really sorry," said Jack. "I didn't realize you were so sensitive and that it bothers you so much when someone argues."

"I am, too! If we stop, will you stay, please? Please! Jack, I promise I'll try very hard not to bug you if you promise not to call me names," said Bangger.

"Yeah, okay, I promise. Now will you stay, Jig? Please. Come on!"

"Okay. Yes! I'll stay, but you better keep your promises," said Jig.

"Great, it wouldn't have been the same without you, Jig," said Jack.

"You mean you two wouldn't have lasted the entire trip without beating each other up," said Jig.

"Well, yes, that too," mumbled Jack.

"Okay! Now that we're all a big happy family once more, shall we get started?" asked Firecracker, watching his newfound friends staring at him.

"The way I figured, we could be at the restaurant by nine thirty. There's a path that leads to the railroad tracks up ahead about fifty feet. We'll follow the path and take the tracks until they come out to a clearing. When we see the lake off to the right, this is where we'll hop on the barge. Once we're on board, you'll see a huge wooden box.

That's where the captain puts all his papers. There is a large hole at the bottom, and this is where I go just in case he brings his cat with him."

"Hey, no one mentioned anything about a cat being on board," said Jig, looking puzzled.

"Don't worry; he can't get to us in there."

"Jacky, are you okay with this?" asked Jig.

"Yes, I think so; he seems like a good guy."

"Are you sure it's not that warm breakfast that's clouding your judgment? You weren't too thrilled with him last night. I don't think he's too worried, Jack; he's got that big stinger. Have you seen the size of that thing?"

"Yeah, I've seen it," said Jack, staring at it.

"I heard legend has it that if they use their stinger once, that's supposed to be the end of them," said Jig, shaking his head, feeling uneasy.

"Gee, that would be a horrible way to go, wouldn't it?" said Jack, rolling his shoulders.

"Yeah, it would really make you think about getting angry with someone. Maybe you should have one, Jack."

"Very funny, Jig."

"Sorry, I'm just joking!"

Firecracker interrupted Jack and Jig talking and continued with his plans.

"As soon as the barge pulls up to the dock on the other side of the lake, we'll make a fast exit to the left," said Firecracker.

"Why's that?" asked Jig curiously.

"Well, there's just one little thing I forgot to mention. Hawks."

Firecracker smiled.

"What do you mean hawks? Do you mean the ones that fly?"

"Is there any other kind? Gee, where did you get your education, out behind the barn?" said Firecracker.

"I suppose you were the top spelling bee?" replied Jack.

"Guys, guys, come on now; lighten up," yelled Jig.

"Fine; what's next?" asked Jack, sizing Firecracker up.

"Well, after we leave the dock, it's about two kilometers east, and just beyond the playground is the restaurant, which to me spells breakfast. I'm just buzzing to get there so let's get a move on. Are you coming?"

"Yup, right behind you." Bangger grimaced.

"Bangger, you shouldn't eat all those berries before breakfast," said Jack.

"Why?"

"I don't know; I just don't think you should."

"Doesn't sound like a good enough reason for me. Hey, Jig, open your mouth. I'll toss you one."

"No, thanks."

"What about you, Firecracker?"

"Sure, I'll try it. Yuk, that's awful. You got to be out of your mind to eat something like that," said Firecracker as he was spitting it out on the ground.

"Ha!" laughed Bangger. "You probably eat too much junk and don't know what's good for you."

"Yeah, well, I'll have you know, every morning I have my tea with honey.

That's good for me."

"What are you doing? Why do you have your ear on the track?"

"I'm listening for the train," said Firecracker.

"Yeah right, sure you are! And I was born today!" snickered Bangger.

"Watch out! Look, up ahead," yelled Jig.

"Holy cow, how did you know that? I guess you really are smart," said Jack, looking puzzled.

"Wow, that train really goes fast," said Bangger, still wondering how Firecracker knew.

"Yup, sure does. Look, guys, over to the right. It should take us about fifteen minutes to climb down the hill to reach the barge."

"Bangger, what are you doing?" asked Jack.

"I'm just going to wrap myself into a ball and then roll all the way down to the bottom of the hill," said Bangger. "That way, I'll get there sooner."

"Jig, look at him go. It really does seem like fun," said Jack, laughing so much he nearly fell over.

"Wee! Come on, guys; try it. It's great," Bangger chuckled.

Looking around at each other, Jack finally said, "Come on, guys; let's do it."

Jack handed his rake to Jig and followed Bangger down the hill.

"Wow, amazing! Come on, fellows. What a hoot!" shouted Jack as he tumbled over a few rocks.

"You go ahead, Jig. I'll fly down with the rake. See you at the bottom," said Firecracker.

Chapter 6

"That was great. I can't remember the last time I had so much fun."

"Feels good, doesn't it, Jig?"

"Yeah, sure does."

"Look, guys; there's the barge. Follow me. Stay close," said Firecracker.

"How are we getting up there?" asked Jig.

"Hold on to my stinger, and I'll pull you up." Firecracker smiled.

"No way. I'm not touching that thing," said Jig, hiding behind Jack.

"It's okay. It won't bite you unless I make it. Come on; it's the only way up." said Firecracker.

"Here, let me go first," said Jack, hoping Firecracker was telling the truth.

"Great view from up here," said Jack, realizing one of his dreams was being fulfilled. "I always wanted to fly."

"Sure is, Jack. When I drop you, head straight over to that wooden box to the right, okay? I'll go back for the others."

"Thanks for the lift, Firecracker," said Jack.

"The pleasure is all mine." Firecracker smiled.

"Are you sure that thing is not going to bite me? I mean, I'm probably allergic to bee stings and I'll more than likely swell up as big as Bangger. And worse than that, I'll probably, well, you know, die or something, and then you'll die, too, because you stung me. Then where would that leave us but to fall from the sky?" said Jig, wiping the sweat from his brow.

"Will you please hush up and take a hold of my stinger?" said Firecracker, tired of flapping his wings.

"Maybe you should give him a little bit of a bite just to get him going," laughed Bangger.

"Why don't you be quiet, Bangger! You think you're so high and mighty," said Jig.

"Testy, testy, aren't we, Jig?" snickered Bangger.

"Are you ready?" asked Firecracker. "Just close your eyes and count to ten, and we'll be there before you know it. Hold on tight."

"Okay, are we there yet?"

"Almost," Firecracker laughed.

"Gee, Jig, I never knew you were such a baby. I heard you all the way over from here," said Jack.

"I'm going back for Bangger; you two stay in the wooden box, out of sight," said Firecracker.

"I need a few minutes to rest before we take off again, Bangger; after that ordeal with Jig, I'm pooped," said Firecracker.

"That's okay; I want to finish my piece of cheese," said Bangger.

A few minutes passed, and then Firecracker and Bangger started out to join the other boys waiting on the barge.

"Jack, when I was up in the sky, I felt like Mighty Mouse," giggled Bangger.

"I'll bet you did, Bangger," laughed Jack.

"How long will it take to reach the other side?" asked Jig.

"It should take about forty minutes," answered Firecracker.

"I'm very nervous thinking about reaching the dock, Jack," said Jig.

"Yes, so am I. Why don't you have a rest, and I'll call you when we're getting close?" said Jack.

"Yes, I think I will. Bangger has flaked out already. So has Firecracker. He was having a hard time pulling Bangger up. I thought he was going to drop him. No wonder he's tired."

As everyone settled for a nap, Jack sat thinking to himself. He didn't want the others to know how upset he was at the thought of reaching the other side of the lake. He heard a lot about hawks and how they were so quick to dive down and pick up their prey.

"What if … No! I can't think like that; I won't. We'll be okay. Surely this bee knows what he is doing."

It wasn't long before Jack heard the whistle blow. It would take a couple of minutes before they reached the dock. Calling to everyone, Jack made sure he had a smile on his face. He knew he had to hide his feelings about being afraid of what could happen with the hawks on the other side of the lake.

"Are you ready, guys?" asked Jack, taking a deep breath.

"Yeah, let's go," said Bangger.

"I'll go first, then you, Jig, Bangger next, and Jack, you can go last," said Firecracker.

"I don't want to go second; you go, Jack," said Jig.

"Fine, then, you can go last."

"No way!"

"Well, then, you had better stay where Firecracker told you to."

"Remember, as soon as we get off the dock, head for that hollow log, run inside, and stay there. Okay, take a deep breath, ready, go. Run, guys, run fast.

Watch out! There's a hawk! Duck! Keep running!"

"Ouch! Help! Help! I fell!"

"Hang on, Bangger; I'm coming. No, leave him alone; let him go!" yelled Jack.

Jack watched as the hawk swarmed down and picked up Bangger after he fell.

"Jack, Jack, help me! Please, help me!"

"I can't, Bangger; I can't reach you!"

Just as quickly as Firecracker made sure Jig got to the other side safely, he went tearing after the hawk that held Bangger captive. Jack raced across the dock waving his rake so the hawk couldn't pick him up. Just as he reached the log, he watched the hawk let go of Bangger. Within seconds, Bangger landed softly on a bed of clover. He got up and ran to the log, looking back to see where Firecracker was.

Up in the sky, the hawk and Firecracker were in a battle. The three mice looked on from the cracks in the hollow log. After a few minutes, the hawk flew away, and they witnessed Firecracker's limp little body floating slowly to the ground.

Inside the log, the three mice sat crying over the loss of their new friend.

They stayed in the hollow log long enough for the other hawks to disappear.

Nobody was thinking of food at the moment.

When they felt it was safe, Jack, Jig and Bangger went over to say goodbye to their friend Firecracker. As they laid blades of grass over him, Jig said a few words.

It didn't take them long after they started out toward the restaurant to reach their destination. While sitting at the restaurant, thinking of what to do next, Jack made a confession to Bangger.

"Bangger, there was a time that I thought I would never say I'm sorry and mean it. After almost losing you today, I have to tell you I really am sorry for all the nasty things I said to you," said Jack, feeling guilty.

"Ah, that's all right, Jack. Does this mean we're buddies?"

"Yes, I guess so." Jack smiled.

"Halleluiah," shouted Jig as he realized everyone could get along.

Chapter 7

Jack laughed, got up, and went for a walk and heard a familiar voice. He looked around the corner and couldn't believe his eyes. There, right in front of him, was Firecracker, stretched out on a banana peel, chomping away on a cheese muffin.

Jack waved to the other boys, and they came running.

"Hi, boys. What took you so long?" said Firecracker as he slapped his knee.

"Firecracker, we thought, well, you know," said Jig.

"What, that I was a goner? Being a yellow jacket, I can sting more than once. I got lots of power; it just exhausts me when I have to use it. You really did get your education out behind the barn," laughed Firecracker.

"Dig in, guys, there's lots to eat. The food's fine, the music is great, and we can relax after under the tree for a nap."

"Hey, Firecracker, do you want to see me do the jig?" asked Jig.

"What! You got to be kidding; you dance?" asked Firecracker.

"Just watch; this is how I earn money, too," laughed Jig.

As everyone watched Jig, Bangger picked up the coins that were tossed.

Although the morning sun popped in and out behind the clouds, the warm summer breeze flowed gently under the branches, bringing the sweet smell of roses with it. It was a day that would be remembered for a long time and would be a mouse tale to be passed on to future generations.

Jack knew now that when Firecracker said he thought it would be the start of a wonderful friendship, he was right. As the boys lay down in the early afternoon for a nap, they were already talking about the next adventure they would be taking. Where, how, and when were three words that crossed their minds. And they also knew that their newfound friend would be joining them.

The End

A Change in Fairyland

In a faraway place known as Fairyland, only good prevailed. Through thousands of years, there had been no evil or misbehaving fairies. In fact, it was so good here that Mother Fairy decided one day to clone and have two of everything. For example, there were two blue fairies, two shoe fairies, two tree fairies, two bee fairies, and everything you could possibly see, there were two of. With each set of fairies came a set of chores. And with their chores came a tradition. To keep the peace in the land, the same two fairies had to either work at a different time of day or in a different direction. It was Belle, the yellow fairy, who started the mornings off as she had been doing for thousands of years. Belle would be the first one up to greet the morning sun and make her rounds to welcome everyone to a brand-new day.

One morning, Belle woke up just a little earlier and was feeling as though something was not quite right. She climbed out of her double bed, looked at the double fruit in the double baskets, jumped out of her mushroom cap, and then landed safely on the grass below. She quickly got up and dusted off her double wings and started on her way.

"Good morning, double trees; good morning, double bees."

"Good morning to you, Belle. Did you sleep well?"

"I did. I'm touched; thank you so much!"

Around the corner she did fly, running into double owls flying by.

"How was your night under the moon? Did you meet up with double raccoons?"

Belle took to flight and was on her way and flew past double houses down by double bays.

Rainbow double fairies were a delight to see, doubling up on colors one, two, three.

"Good morning, double blue fairies. Please don't be sad. There are more friends to make double glad.

"Good morning, double shoe fairies. You work really fast.

Doubling up on leather to make the shoes last."

"Thank you, Belle. You're so sweet, but when are you going to bring Ann around for us to meet?"

"All in good time," she said as she waved her wand. Looking down, she spotted double fishes in double ponds.

"Hello there, double boats. Will you set sail, going in different directions to deliver the mail?"

With all her good mornings out of the way, Belle flew home to start her day.

Like always, Belle went straight to Ann's cap, to wake her up from her morning nap.

As she tilted her mushroom down to the ground, she peeked inside and did not hear a sound.

Over by the double chairs and pinned on the double beds, there were two ransom notes, and this is what they said.

Each one was written in double inks of red and blue, and they said, "If you want to see Ann again, you will have to change a thing or two."

With double haste, without any waste, she took the notes over to double owls' place.

Belle thought that two birds were better than one. "Can you please help me? Last night, did you see anyone?"

With double hoots and double sighs, they both looked at Belle and said, "Oh my! We started playing a double game of Scrabble, which we didn't mention. We're really sorry; it wasn't our intention."

Belle walked away with her head turned down, and then she spotted it on the ground.

There were specks of double red and blue, and she realized she found her first double clue.

She followed it for quite some time. If she could figure it out, she could solve this crime.

Up and down she used her double eyes; looking all around from side to side.

Belle was thinking that whoever took Ann was not very smart, leaving a trail, almost from the start.

Into the bush a little further she walked, her voice getting lower as she talked.

Double eyes were glowing all around, shifting from side to side without a sound.

Slowly with each step Belle did go, passing double moles and double trolls, going down in double holes.

All of a sudden, Belle found double clue two, a piece of Ann's double wing, because it was yellow not blue.

She saw double footprints over to the right and decided to follow them, then came to a light.

There on the path up ahead was a shadow; it could be very scary, down here in the meadow.

Belle thought to herself, "I can't go alone." She really got frightened when she heard a big moan.

"I'll go home and gather up all doubles to help me find Ann, who is in a lot of trouble."

Off she went and found double bees. "Can you ask everyone to come with me?

"Please, double fishes, swim upstream; she may be thirsty. Double cows, please bring double cream.

"Double ropes; there are still lots of hope. We'll need double length; pulling together will give us double strength.

"There is one place I didn't look in the cave on the other side of the brook.

"I didn't think they would take her there because of double old grouchy bears."

Double fishes Art and Dave swam up the stream under the cave.

They came to the surface and, in delight, were shocked to see Ann dancing in the light.

"Oh! How naughty you were to misbehave. Wait until Belle gets here; then what are you going to say?"

"It doesn't matter what she'll say. I know I'm right; and just to let you know, I'm tired of saying good night."

"What is it that you would like to do? You should have gone to talk with double mother and double father, too!"

"I'm sure they would have asked if we could take turns; it probably would have been good for everyone concerned."

At the entrance to the cave at the very top, Belle waited patiently for double bears to take a double nap.

She knew they were sleeping when they let out a big sigh. Slowly and steadily she slipped on by.

Over the cracks and down through the holes, with double beeswax candles she did go.

She called out to Art and Dave, the double fish, "Won't someone answer me?

That is my wish."

"We're down here, Belle, near the sand, at the bottom of the cave, and we did find Ann."

With a flick of her wings and a toss of her wand, it didn't take her long to fly to the ground.

"Oh! Ann, are you all right? You had me scared; and where is the bad fairy that put you down here?"

With Ann's head hung low and not much to say, double fishes told Belle what happened that day.

Belle was disappointed but knew what she meant. She thought many times about changing tradition a bit.

"We'll go home and converse with the others. We'll draw up a petition and present it to Mother."

They found that some things are good, staying the same, and sometimes you need change in order to gain.

"You can have my job first thing in the day; you can hear them wake up with something to say.

"You can also hear how rude they can be, and a lot of times they throw food at me."

"Oh, hold it right there. I have changed my mind; I am better suited for nighttime.

I promise to be good and will never run again, and I guess I'll have to make some kind of amends."

"I'm sorry, Ann, but you will have to pay and scrub double toilets until the end of May."

"Oh no, the toilets I just couldn't do, anything but that. I'll throw up in my shoe."

For all the thousands of years before, not a single fairy misbehaved and worried everyone more.

And for all the years still to come, let us hope our Ann will be the only one!

The End

Friends

Jillie the witch was a mischievous little girl.

She had long wispy hair and one big curl.

All over town she would fly on her broom, making a mess in all the kids' rooms.

One by one, they all got into trouble.

Jillie with gum would blow a big bubble.

It was stuck on the bedposts, lampshades, and clothes, and even in the morning, it was stuck on their toes.

Down to breakfast the children would go, through hallways and doorways all in a row.

The children explained to their parents one night that it was Jillie doing this because of a fight.

All the parents just laughed and said, "Don't be silly.

There's no such person as a witch named Jillie."

But the children knew better and thought of a way, to get even with Jillie on this day.

They gathered up carrots, spaghetti, and apple juice, along with marshmallows, gum drops, and strawberry mousse.

They all took turns stirring the pot, and each one knew what the other one thought.

With carrot sticks rolled in her hair and marshmallows, and juice everywhere, they knew for sure they would get a laugh and for weeks to come she'd have to soak in the bath.

The spaghetti was there to tie her broom, so she could not fly up to the moon.

The gumdrops would be given at the very end if she agreed to be a friend.

"Oh," thought the children, "how she would look if someone took a picture for a book."

They were laughing so much they fell on the ground over and over and rolled around and around.

Just before the children got going, along came Jillie with a wagon towing.

It was filled with notes for all the kids, telling them she was sorry for what she did.

The children felt bad and apologized, too, for making fun of Jillie's pointed shoes.

They were the best friends she ever had, and the children took her home to meet Mom and Dad.

The End

Who Are You?

"Who are you beneath my old spruce tree? I know you're there; I just can't see."

In the quiet of night, I heard the sounds. I grabbed the flashlight and looked all around.

I got out of bed and rubbed my eyes. The noise I heard came from outside.

I hurried to the window, and in the dark I saw a tiny light under my old spruce tree.

Tonight I decided to sneak a peek, between the branches, hoping to meet whoever it was that made his home under my tree all alone.

Across the lawn I tiptoed with care, anxiously wondering who was there.

On my knees I bent down to look. Guess what I saw reading a book.

A little old man with a beard of white. I knew if he saw me, he'd duck out of sight.

With his little brown cap and his crooked nose, he wore big yellow shoes that curled at the toes.

His shirt was orange, and his pants were blue, held up with suspenders that were really cool.

I watched him just for a little while, and then suddenly I noticed a wee funny smile.

He jerked to the left and then to the right. Snapping his fingers, he disappeared from sight.

As I sat on the grass, I wondered if he would come again under my old spruce tree.

I rose to my feet, and a horn I did hear. I turned around and was sure someone was near.

I took a few steps, and out of the blue, across my head came a little yellow shoe.

I called out to him, "You shouldn't do that! Maybe you would like to meet my big black cat."

He didn't show up for the rest of the night, and I hung his shoe right next to the light.

I hurried back to bed to get some rest, and then I saw my room; what a mess!

I knew where he went when he disappeared. Straight to my room, that's very clear.

The sun came up as I laid my head down. Within a few minutes, Mother was making her rounds.

She called out to me five or six times, "Get up, Master Cameron; it's almost nine."

"But, Mom, I'm too tired. I need some sleep. I just can't get up. I don't want anything to eat."

"Never mind, my son. If you can't go to school, there'll be no swimming later for you, in the pool."

"Oh! All right, I will get up and go. I'm not very pleased with that little old troll.

Today I'll find him if it takes me all night. I'll look under everything with all my might.

I'm going to let him know who, is the boss, and if he doesn't like it, he can go get lost."

I went off to school, and later that day, my friend asked, "Why don't you come over to play?"

I told him, "I can't; I have to go home." I was on a mission, all alone.

Although I was tired, I needed to be out on the lawn watching under my tree.

I sat there for hours and heard Mother call. I got up to leave and saw the ball.

It came rolling out from under the tree, and then I thought, "Maybe he wants to be friends with me!"

I dropped to my knees and looked underneath the tree to find two huge teeth.

His smile was horrible and so were his eyes. It scared me so badly I wanted to cry.

I jumped up quickly and started to run; and then he yelled, "Will you be my friend? I want to play with someone!"

I stopped in my tracks and turned around, and on his face was one big frown.

I looked at him with fright in my eyes, and somehow I knew he wasn't scary inside.

He whimpered a bit and said, "Don't be afraid; I only changed because of a raid.

I'm not really old and horrible to see. I'm a handsome young lad, and a spell was put on me.

I came from a world far away. I didn't want to leave, but I just couldn't stay.

Everyone was sad except for me. I just couldn't take it, so I decided to flee.

I had no idea where to go. I've never been away from Bubble Land Cove.

It's a place where happiness begins, and all the children burst bubbles with pins.

The air in the bubbles was the color of mauve. It spread like a blanket all over the cove.

It kept everyone happy, no troubles or fears. It had been carried on for thousands of years.

One day, a stranger came into town. He was mean to everyone that was around.

He was quite a bit bigger than all of us. He took our bubbles and made a mess.

He ordered all the people to stop being glad and said, 'From now on, you all will be sad.'

Our world sure changed when sadness prevailed. I was the only one to challenge him, and then I set sail.

Before I left, he cast a spell on me and said, 'Now you're a troll living under a tree.'

As I listened to him, I just couldn't believe how someone so nice could be treated so mean.

He continued to tell me not to be afraid. He said, "I'm really desperate, and I'm in need of aid."

In spite of his looks, I wasn't scared. I asked him how I could help and that I really did care.

He asked me if I was frightened to fly, and I told him we didn't do that and we shouldn't try.

He looked at me puzzled and said, "Don't you believe? Just close your eyes and you will see."

He took my hand and tapped it twice. Around in a circle we ran like mice.

"Keep your eyes closed or you'll break your thought. We'll be there in a moment at the town clock."

When we arrived, he said, "Open your eyes ... You just have to believe; it doesn't matter who you are or your size."

We flew back to my house, and on that day, I found a friend not far away.

I hurried home from school to play and share my treats with him each day.

Within a short few weeks, I knew something was bothering him. He left a clue.

His happy spirit turned to sad, and I found out why he wasn't glad.

He talked about how he missed Bubble Land Cove and all its bliss.

I asked him how I could help him go home, so he wouldn't feel so all alone.

He said it would take more than two to break the spell and send him through.

Right away, I knew who to pick: my sister, Emma. That would do the trick.

She believed in fairies and all that was good. With her on our team, we surely could.

I ran to call her and found that she had already known about my troll and tree.

She agreed to help me with my friend. Saying goodbye was a horrible end.

As we stood side by side, we had no idea we were going for a ride.

He said, think happy thoughts as we close our eyes. United together we will fly."

It didn't take us long to get to his land, with eyes closed, hand in hand.

When we arrived, he said, "Open your eyes." I couldn't believe it; what a surprise!

Everything was pink and blue, green and yellow and purple, too.

All the cats and all the dogs belonged to everyone, even the hogs.

With grumpy faces all around, it must have been terrible to live in this town.

Down the road I walked and heard a nasty person stating the law.

I yelled out to him, "You stop right there! Enough of that nonsense. Don't you care?"

He stopped in his tracks and said, "Who are you? You can't tell me what to do."

I replied, "I will, wait and see. You're no longer boss here, says me.

I came from another world to help my friend. We are going to change Bubble Land Cove back again."

I gathered the people all over town to put an end to this big nasty clown.

In a great big circle we did stand, holding on to one another's hand.

"Close your eyes and you must believe. Think happy things, and you will see.

To make someone nasty disappear, we had to stand together, this was clear."

As we opened our eyes, the spell was broken. The raid was over, and no words were spoken.

The bubbles were released and pricked with a pin. All over the town it was mauve again.

The happy moods were here to stay, and Emma and I were on our way.

Just before we closed our eyes, my little friend came to say goodbye.

"How can I pay you for what you've done?"

"That's very nice, but a thank you is all that's needed for helping someone.

I hope you'll visit us again. It's been great having you for a friend.

Take care for now. We're on our way, happy thoughts of love today.

Back at home, I'm sure to see how friendship means the world to me.

It doesn't matter what you find; love is always good and kind.

Goodbye today from Emma and me. We'll see you next time under our tree!"

The End

Peter Hawk Rabbit and the Last Laugh

Peter Hawk Rabbit lived across the field from Grandpa Harry and Grandma Jean Rabbit. Although they had the same last name, they were not related. Peter had set out on an adventure, leaving his home at Furland Farms on the East Coast. When he arrived here at Bunnies Bay, he was greeted with friendliness. For the past two years, Peter had enjoyed himself, taking advantage of the townspeople. He had been given a middle name that suited him perfectly, and he was proud of it. Every once in a while, Peter would snitch something, and that's how he acquired the name Hawk.

For three days, Peter had been hiding behind the tool shed watching closely, waiting for Grandma Jean to bake her pies. Today was Thursday, and he started to get worried because he hadn't seen any in the usual place. He decided to take a nap, and when he woke up, the sweet smell of carrot pies was heading his way. Watching for Grandpa Harry to disappear into the root cellar, Peter made his way over to the window ledge and grabbed the pies.

"Come back here, Peter Hawk Rabbit. You can't take my pies this year!" yelled Grandma Jean. From around the corner, Grandpa came running to see what all the fuss was about.

"Is everything all right?" asked Grandpa.

"Peter snitched my pies," said Grandma. "I can't believe that he actually did it again."

"Should I go after him?" questioned Grandpa.

"No, it's okay. I made a double batch this year because I thought he might try it again," said Grandma Jean.

Grandma was upset with Peter taking her pies, but she also knew that this would be the best year at the county fair.

Running away as fast as he could with Grandma's famous carrot pies, Peter looked over his shoulder to make sure no one was following him. When he reached the other side of the cornfield, Peter knew he had once again pulled off the biggest joke of the year; only this time, someone had seen him. Just as soon as he got home with them, Peter stored the pies in a container and put them in the refrigerator.

Once again, Peter thought how smart he was, getting away with taking something that didn't belong to him.

Peter thought that today was an adventure in its own. Half of the fun was stealing the pies. Last year, he won the county fair baking contest with Grandma's pies. This year, he was going to do the same thing and looked forward to having a great day tomorrow.

As evening approached, Peter wondered why no one came to confront him about taking the pies when he knew Grandma Jean had seen him.

He quickly dismissed it and laid his clothes out for morning. After watching television, he washed his face, brushed his teeth, and hopped into bed.

Upon waking the next morning, Peter jumped into the shower, brushed his long ears till they shone, quickly got dressed, and put on his big green and purple bowtie that he won last year at the fair.

When he was finished, Peter went downstairs to retrieve the basket for the pies.

Just as he was taking them out of the fridge, in came his friend Chatter, a blue jay.

"What have you got there?" asked Chatter.

"It's my pies for the baking contest," said Peter.

"Where did you get them this year, Peter?" asked Chatter, snickering.

"I didn't get them anywhere. I made them," said Peter, sounding annoyed.

"Yeah right, and my name is Pumpkin Pie and I bake jelly," laughed Chatter.

"You can laugh all you want, but when I win the baking contest, I won't be sharing treats with you," said Peter.

"Well, if that's the way you feel, fine. I'm going. I'll see you later at the fair," said Chatter as he stomped off.

"Wait up, Chatter; I thought we could walk together. After all, it's a nice fall day," said Peter.

"Why should I? You don't want to share with me, and that's not very nice," replied Chatter.

"You should trust me when I tell you I baked them," Peter said, crossing his fingers behind his back. "After all, you sure enjoyed the treats we bought last year with the prize money from the contest. I watched how you gobbled up those peanuts. If you want more this year, you need to keep your mouth closed and just go along with what I tell you," said Peter, showing anger.

"That's fine, Peter, but I know the truth, and it's not nice to lie or steal." Chatter frowned.

"Maybe it's not, but has anyone tried to stop me or say anything? No. So until they do, I'll just do as I please," announced Peter.

"Okay, Peter, but remember, you can only get away with pulling pranks for so long," said Chatter.

"Yeah well, we'll see," laughed Peter. "That's enough about this! Look at all the beautiful trees. I like the red leaves the best. Did you see that chipmunk over there near the hollow log?" asked Peter.

"He looks like the same one that took all my nuts last year," said Chatter. "I'm sure of it, because I remember when I went after him, I pulled out his fur at the end of his tail; see how it's missing?"

"Talk about me! Don't you think it's wrong to harm someone else, especially over nuts?" asked Peter.

"It's no worse than taking something from others that doesn't belong to you.

You're still hurting someone," snapped Chatter.

"I think it is, and anyway, this conversation is over!" yelled Peter.

"Fine. I'm leaving, and you can find your own way to the fair. Goodbye," said Chatter as he flew off.

"I don't need his help anyway. I know my way to the fair. When I win that money, I'm going to buy the biggest carrot I can find and maybe a few heads of lettuce.

Then I'm going to play some games and try to win one of those big yellow hats that they have every year, and if I don't win, maybe I'll just take it." Peter smiled. "Wow, here comes Jess.

She's a sweet bunny. She makes my heart sing, and look at those big green eyes.

"Good morning, Jess. Are you going to the fair?" asked Peter.

"Yes, I am, and I don't care to walk with you," answered Jess.

"I don't care either, and what's wrong with everyone today?" asked Peter.

"What's wrong? Why don't you ask yourself? You used to be a nice rabbit until you started to take things that were not yours. How many times are you going to do this?

Don't you care? You hurt a lot people over the last couple of years," said Jess.

"I'm not hurting anyone. I'm just having fun," snickered Peter.

"Gee, look, it's Grandpa and Grandma Rabbit," said Jess. "Hi!"

"I have to go. See you at the fair, Jess," said Peter, hopping toward the path to the fairground.

Up ahead on the right was a small bridge that Peter had to cross over to get to the big tent where the judging would take place. Once he reached the other side, Peter hid behind a small bush. Grandpa Harry said, "Good luck," to Grandma Jean as she entered the tent with the other contestants. He told her that he was on his way over to the horseshoe toss, hoping to bring back the first prize ribbon as he had done for the past four years.

Peter watched as Grandpa disappeared from sight. He knew that it would take at least thirty minutes before all the judges were ready to start. Straightening his bowtie and fluffing his tail, Peter took a deep breath. He had a smile on him as long as his ears.

Holding his basket proudly, he walked through the front entrance of the tent whistling.

All eyes were on him as he reached the table where he would lay his pies out for judging. He felt a little uneasy because no one was speaking to him. Out of the corner of his eye, he spotted his friend Chatter and thought maybe he had said something to the people who were judging the contest. After seeing the look on Chatter's face, Peter knew he had not turned him in.

The judges this year were Rusty Rooster from Rounds River, Belinda Bear from Barrel Beans and also, the twins June and Jerry from Jumping Jersey. The panel of judges was selected three months in advance, and no one knew who they were until that day.

Peter glanced across the room to find Grandma Jean smiling and waving to him.

He waved back, still wondering why she had not said anything to him about the pies.

His thoughts were interrupted when he saw the judges coming. They started at the other end of the table and slowly made their way down toward him. With each bite they took, Peter was getting more nervous as he watched the smiles that came across their faces. He could faintly hear them saying how good they were and that all of them so far had a very good chance of winning. Peter's knees were shaking as the judges stood in front of him.

Never before had he felt like this, and at this moment, he was unsure of himself. He managed to put a big smile on his face and watched curiously as the first judge sampled the pie.

"Yuk! What do you call this?" asked Belinda. "June, Jerry, come over here and taste this."

"What is it?" said June and Jerry.

"Don't ask me. I can smell it from here," said Rusty as he made a terrible face.

"Whatever do you mean? What's wrong with my pie?" questioned Peter.

"What's the main ingredient in your pie, Peter?" asked Jerry.

"Well, it's … it's … I forget," said Peter. "Maybe you should try the other one."

"Go ahead, Rusty; we've done our duty," said Belinda.

"I can't. It smells like vinegar, and I hate vinegar!" yelled Rusty. "You try it."

"Give me a taste of those pies," screamed Peter as he took a spoonful from the first one and then tried the second.

Within seconds, Peter spit the pies out on the ground, cursing. Covering up his embarrassment, he quickly turned on the other contestants saying they switched his pies when he wasn't looking. Everyone knew that Peter was telling a lie. The judges made a decision and chose Maryanne's and Grandma Jean's pies. It was the first tie in all the years of the county fair.

Through the crowd, Grandma Jean came running, laughing so much that Peter's ears turned a bright pink because he was embarrassed.

"Well, Peter, what do you have to say for yourself?" asked Grandma Jean.

"Maybe now you won't be so eager to take things that don't belong to you. This time, it is not you who gets the last laugh but the rest of us in Bunnies Bay. I hope we can be friends the way friends are supposed to be. Around here, we help each other and respect others' properties. Stealing and telling lies can get you into a lot of trouble."

Grandma Jean turned and walked outside to meet Grandpa Harry, leaving Peter behind. As she headed over to where he had been tossing horseshoes, she saw Grandpa coming toward her, waving a bright red ribbon and carrying a brass horseshoe. They gave each other a hug and walked arm in arm along the path to reach home. They exchanged stories, and Grandpa knew why she didn't want him to go after Peter that day he took her pies.

The look on Peter's face was priceless when he found out that the biggest joke of the year turned out to be on him. Grandma knew that this was one Rabbit County Fair she would remember for a long time.

And as for Peter Hawk Rabbit, he learned a very valuable lesson, one that would take a lot of energy to try to make up for all the wrong he had done in the past. His first stop was at the home of Grandpa and Grandma Rabbit to apologize.

The End

Melting Lands

As we walked up to the front of Melting Lands Public School, I was excited because this would be my first time going to a real school. There were lots of trees to shade us from the sun and keep the cold wind out in winter. At the side of the building stood a big arch that looked like a rainbow that had melted. It was painted many colors, too!

Grandpa walked slowly with me as we made our way into the school. We had to go to the office so I could get registered for classes. After talking to the vice principal, I said goodbye to Grandpa and was introduced to a student named Jim who came to take me to my new classroom. As the door opened, all eyes turned on me, and I was a little frightened of going in. A nice lady by the name of Ms. Barns came over and took my hand and led me to the front of the class. Jim told her my name, and she introduced me to the rest of my classmates. Ms. Barns, my teacher, welcomed me to her class and asked me to have a seat next to the window. I listened to some of the other students giving a speech. I was told that everyone in her class had to give one. I was very nervous and hoped she wouldn't ask me.

The morning went fast, and as I headed outside with my lunchbox, a girl who was in my class came to talk to me. Her name was Vanessa. We had lunch together and then played ball with a group of other kids.

When the bell rang, we went back into the classroom, and Ms. Barns called me up to her desk. She told me that she would like me to do my speech on Thursday.

I said, "Yes," and walked over to sit down. I sat all afternoon thinking about this and wondered what I would give a speech on. Just as I heard the bell ring, it came to me. I could write a speech on my travels with Grandpa. I rushed home to ask Grandpa if it would be all right. He thought it was a great idea, so I sat down with a pencil and paper and started to write down everything I could think of before we came to Melting Lands.

Tuesday and Wednesday went quickly. I went to bed early, but I didn't sleep very well because I was so nervous about giving my speech the next day. I knew it would be my turn after lunch. Amanda and Michael went first. I sat anxiously tossing my pencil up and down, hoping Ms. Barns would forget me. The moment I heard her call my name, I had knots in my stomach, and they seemed to go right up to my throat. With every step I took toward the front of the class, I felt faint. I took a deep breath, and just as I was about to start, the door opened and in walked Grandpa. Ms. Barns motioned for him to come over and sit with her. For some reason, seeing him gave me the confidence I needed to tell my story. I looked at Grandpa, and he winked, and I knew everything would be okay.

I cleared my throat and started my speech.

Ms. Barns and fellow classmates, my story is about riding the trains with my grandpa and my dog, Sam. When I was four years old, I lost my parents in a car accident.

My grandfather became my guardian.

He worked with a circus that traveled throughout the country. We lived in a trailer and moved with the circus from town to town. When I was big enough, I joined the circus, too. I was a clown dressed in blue and orange stripes with red hair.

My name was Smiley because I had the biggest smile of all the clowns. My grandpa was known as the king of clowns, and everyone enjoyed his act the best.

Although we had jobs, I still had to go to school. Every day from eleven o'clock to two thirty, a retired schoolteacher would come to our trailer to tutor me. Grandpa was very strict about my schooling.

One day, I overheard the owner, Mr. Caplock, tell his friend he was going to sell the circus. I ran home and told Grandpa what I had heard, and he went to confront him.

They had words, and my grandfather told Mr. Caplock we would not be staying on after Saturday. I felt really bad, but Grandpa said it was not my fault. The next morning, we packed up some of our things and waited patiently for Saturday to arrive. At the end of the show, Grandpa asked John to give us a lift over to the train station. He sat in the front, and I sat in the back with my dog, Sam. We said goodbye to John and boarded the train.

At first, it was fun traveling with my grandpa, going first east then west. Grandpa was looking for work, hopefully with another circus. His second choice was working in a post office, which he did as a young man growing up until he decided to join the circus.

This is where he met my grandma. Grandpa told me that my grandma was the apple of his eye and he loved her very much. He also said that one day she got sick and died of a terrible disease.

It started to get chilly at night because fall was getting close, and it was near the end of summer.

Every day, Grandpa would pick up a newspaper and go through the want ads trying to find work. It seemed as though there wasn't much hope. We traveled from east to west and then south. Grandpa said that our money was starting to run out, and we would have to ride in the boxcars, so we could save it for food. We weren't sure how long it would be before Grandpa got work.

The last town that we stopped at had an old shed beside the railroad tracks.

Grandpa said that we would rest there while the train switched cars. When no one was looking, we quickly eased up into the boxcar, bolting the door behind us.

It was then that Grandpa said, 'Remember, Ryan, to keep Sam quiet; we want to make sure we stay warm tonight.'

As the whistle blew and the train pulled away from the station, I peeked out between the boards. I saw rings of smoke coming out of the stack, floating up toward the sky. I settled into one corner, using my backpack as a pillow, and Grandpa threw his extra coat over me. Sam nudged his way right up close to my back and snuggled in behind me.

I asked Grandpa where we were headed, and he said we were going up north to a place called Melting Lands. I told him that was a funny name for a town. He said it was named after a metal company that had moved there some years ago. He also told me that once a month trains would bring scrap metal up there to be melted down. I was curious about this place we were going to, but I was also tired and went to sleep.

As I drifted off, I thought about being under the big tent and how I missed it. It was hard not to hear the excitement and laughter from all the people. Part of me wished I was still there. The other part knew I had to trust my grandpa.

He would always make the right decisions for us both.

"As dawn approached, the train's horn blew and woke me up. It was dark inside the boxcar, even though the sun was rising. I sat up and searched in my backpack for a sandwich that I saved from the night before.

When I couldn't find it, I remembered the old flashlight that I had found. I took it out of my pocket and shone the light so I could see. I pulled out my sandwich and shared it with Sam.

When the train stopped, we carefully climbed down off the boxcar and waited for everyone to leave before heading to the general store. I waited outside with Sam for Grandpa to come back out. Around the side of the building, I noticed a board full of help-wanted jobs. I started to read them and came across one that said, 'Donley's Circus in town; clown acts needed.' I couldn't go into the store because of Sam, so just as soon as Grandpa came out, I showed it to him. We were so happy and asked directions to the fairgrounds.

Grandpa met Mr. Garvey, and we both started working that night. He gave us a place to stay while they were in town. It was three weeks before the circus was packing up to leave. Mr. Garvey asked if we would like to come with them, and Grandpa said he needed to stay here and find a place so I could go to school. He thanked us for helping him out and told my grandpa that if he went over to talk to his friend at the post office he just might be able to get a job there. We said, 'Goodbye,' to Mr. Garvey and walked over to the post office to talk with Mrs. Mathews. She was glad that Grandpa had some experience with the mail and hired him right then.

"With the money we saved from Donley's Circus, we had enough to rent a house.

Grandpa and I talked and decided to stay here in Melting Lands. He said I could go to a real school and make friends that I could keep for a long time.

I turned my head and looked over at my grandpa and saw a tear in his eye. At that moment, I knew that the love and trust that we shared would always be with us.

The whole class clapped their hands and said that my story was great. The days of riding the trains were over, and the best part is my grandpa and I are still together along with Sam!

The End

Flataline's Journey

One night while I was sleeping, something woke me up. At first, I thought it was a mouse squeaking, and when I realized it wasn't, I felt a little frightened. It sounded like a tiny human. Then I thought it must be Arthur playing jokes again. It was late, and I was tired, and I was not in the mood for games. All I wanted to do was go back to sleep. I turned around and pulled the blankets over my head. Just as I did, I heard a tiny little voice calling my name.

"Johnny, wake up!"

"Who's there? Arthur, you better stop playing games, or I'm telling Mrs. Tinker. You'll be in big trouble tomorrow." When I went to lie back down, I heard it again. This time, it said, "Johnny, my name is Flataline, and I'm your pillow."

"Okay, Arthur, this time, you have gone too far."

"It's not Arthur, Johnny. It's me, Flataline. I'm your pillow, and I can talk."

I sat up in bed and rubbed my eyes and tried to see who was pulling a prank on me. As I was sitting there, I felt something move behind me. I slowly turned around and saw my pillow dancing. In my surprise,

I backed up, nearly falling off the bed. I began to tremble and could hardly speak. Somehow I managed to get up enough courage to say something and asked, "Who are you, and what do you want with me?" I couldn't believe my ears; this pillow laughed.

Again it said, "Johnny, I'm your pillow, and I can talk. I'm here because you need me just as much as I need you."

"That's it, Arthur. How are you doing this?"

"Johnny, why don't you put on the light, and you'll see who I am," said Flataline.

"Yeah, okay, but if we get caught, you're taking the blame. I don't know how you're doing this, Arthur, but it's a good joke." When I turned on the light, I couldn't believe my eyes; it really was a pillow. "Are you a ghost or something?"

"No. I told you who I was."

"Oh, come on; everyone knows that pillows do not talk. Gee, I hope there is no one listening to me; they might think I've lost my marbles."

"Johnny, do you believe in dreams coming true?"

"Why?"

"Well, I never used to until now. I didn't think I would ever belong to anyone. I'm glad I'm here with you because I can tell you are a nice boy, and I always wished someday I would end up with a kind person. I hoped someone would look after me and not shake my stuffing out. So tell me, do you believe in dreams coming true?"

"I don't know. At one time I thought maybe they could, but not anymore."

"Gee, Johnny, you sound really sad. I used to be sad, too. Do you want to share stories about your life before we met?"

"All right, you go first, because I really don't have much to tell."

"Where should I begin?" Flataline asked.

"Why don't you start at the beginning? Where did you come from, and how did you get here?"

Flataline sat down at the head of the bed and started to tell Johnny her life story.

"A long time ago at the factory where I was born, I was tossed aside because I happened to be flat and not fat.

Mr. Cruthers, the owner of the factory, told his employees not to ship me out with the rest of the pillows because I was not plump. Every week I said goodbye to my friends and hoped I would meet them somewhere in the future. With each passing day, my hope for finding a home became less. As the days grew longer, so did the contracts that Sally,

Mr. Cruthers' daughter had to fill. It was a time of year in which pillows seemed to be in demand.

Just last year, Mr. Cruthers shipped out three thousand white and two thousand colored pillows. Two days before I left, the whole factory was upset. The cutting machine for the pillow cases broke down, and it looked as though Sally couldn't fill the order. She was nineteen pillows short. Mr. Cruthers called a meeting with his employees and asked if everyone would give up their pillows that had been given to them earlier that week. The pillows were all set aside until Friday, and that's when they would take them home along with a bonus for doing a great job.

This was a yearly event. As it was, everyone agreed and knew they would receive two pillows in place of one. Everyone was happy to contribute to the success again by pulling together as a team. After everyone went home on Friday, Sally sat making out the packing slips for shipment. She then realized she was still one pillow short. After talking to her father, she came right over to where I was stuffed in a corner. She picked me up and said, 'Look, Father, I think we could use this pillow to fill the contract.'

I was the exact length and width, and I was white.

Nowhere in the contract did it say a pillow had to be fat; it just mentioned the width and length.

'You're right, Sally. I think we could get by with this. After all, there isn't that much difference.

What a feeling I had, Johnny, when I realized I was the pillow that saved the day for the Cruthers. At that moment, I knew I was on my way to freedom and maybe finding some of my old friends. It was a long ride on the big truck that took me to Mr. Brown's store. After the shipper unloaded us, we sat in a big box for a few days. It was near the end of the week when a young lady came over to sort us out and place us on the shelves. At first, I was very nervous about meeting all my new friends. There were two twin picture frames that were beautiful, Mini the blind, a flower power plate, Crystal Vase, and Holes in the Blanket. It was Holes in the Blanket that I became good friends with. When I sat up on the shelf, I was as proud as a peacock, waiting for someone to pick me up and take me home with them. Everyone who touched me loved how clean and white I was, but when they squeezed me, they put me back on the shelf. I didn't want to get too discouraged, but one day, I was feeling sad because someone said something which was not very nice, and it made me cry. I was so upset I started to sing a song and it went like this: 'Nobody wants to take me home. I'm stuck right here all alone, just because I'm flat not fat. Please don't think I'm some old mat.'

"I was at the store for about six months when Mr. Brown decided to have a sale. He gathered up all the items he couldn't sell and put us in a large bin. On the front was a sign that said, 'If you buy two items from the sale, you can choose another from the bin for free.' At first, I was really happy being there with all my friends, and I met some new ones, too. It was great for a while, and then sadly, I was saying goodbye to them, too.

"I waved at Torn Towel, smiled at Ripped Dishcloth, cried tears of joy for Water-Stained Sheets, and gave Stale Corn Chips a tub of dip as a going-away present.

I looked around and saw my good friend Holes in the Blanket. He was crying, and I went to comfort him. He felt sad, just like me, because we both wanted to belong to someone.

"After the store closed on the last day of the sale, Mr. Brown locked the door and shut off all but one light. It was quiet, and then we heard Mr. Brown pick up the phone and talk to someone.

He told the people on the other end to send a big truck in the morning and then hung up the phone. I hardly slept that night and had an uneasy feeling about what was going to happen in the morning. The next day, Shirley, who worked at the store, arrived early and started to put us all in the big box that was sitting over in the corner. Holes in the Blanket wrapped himself around me so we wouldn't get lost in the shuffle. In the box, we met Plastic Glasses, Orange Peeler, Frayed Carpet, Missing Pages Book, and a game called Keepers. Mini the blind was also there. She had been returned to the store because her strings came undone. When the flaps of the box were folded, Mr. Brown pushed us over to the dock at the back of the store. We heard a doorbell ring, and then two strange men came and picked us up, and we were put on a big truck.

"Everyone was worried because we had heard many stories while being at the store.

Someone told us that if Mr. Brown couldn't sell his stock, sometimes it ended up at the dump. I was afraid maybe that's where we were headed. I kept this to myself and hoped it wasn't one of those times. It was a bumpy ride, and it wasn't long after we started out that we stopped. I peeked out between the flaps of the box and realized we had not been taken to the dump, but we had reached the home of the local orphanage. The huge doors of the truck opened, and we were lifted off the truck.

"A man from inside the building came to tell the men where to put the box we were in.

Once we were inside the building, the two men said goodbye and closed the door. I couldn't see anything because it was dark, but I did hear lots of children. I didn't want to get my hopes up, but I thought to myself that children need pillows and blankets and maybe I'd found a home. The rest of the day, we stayed in the box until nighttime. I was sure everyone had gone to bed because it was dark outside, too. A very nice lady by the name of Mrs. Tinker opened the box and started to take us out. She unraveled Holes in the Blanket to find me. Just then, when everything was quiet, a young boy came running out of his room crying. He sounded heartbroken. Mrs. Tinker asked him what was wrong and he said, 'I can't go to sleep because I don't have a pillow.'

"I lit up like a bright moon and held my breath as Mrs. Tinker pulled me from the box and gave me to you. I was so happy knowing I finally belonged to someone. I waited until we were out of sight from everyone, and I quietly sang a song: 'Someone will love me, this I know, for little Johnny needs me so. I'll be happy, and he will, too. We'll hug each other the whole night through.' "Johnny, that's how I came to be with you. That's my story. What about yours? Johnny, are you going to sleep? Wake up!"

"I'm too tired; I'll tell you another day."

Off to sleep went Flataline, dreaming of all the fun times she would have with Johnny, and she knew she would bring him good luck. Johnny, on the other hand, was thinking that maybe, just maybe, he should believe in dreams coming true. And just like Johnny, you, too, should believe that dreams can come true!

The End

About the Author

Her love for writing started many years ago under an old willow tree and progressed to a fine standing oak. Somewhere between reality and fantasy and her love for children, grew a heart-warming connection to bring forth Magical Journeys.

Friendships meet challenges, overcoming obstacles to restoring love and trust. It is a journey written in, for, and to endure love.

She (the writer) has promised your ride with her into an adventure will leave you wishing to hold onto a child-like innocence for years to come.

The enchanting stories for ages 3 to 99 will take you on a magical journey, one sure to keep a smile on your face long after you have stopped reading.

Printed in the United States
43067LVS00003B/139-228

9 781420 852127